Snow Day Dare

Happy Birthday to
_____Rohan_____
From Mr. Mucci

by ABBY KLEIN

illustrated by
JOHN McKINLEY

Scholastic Inc.

ISBN 978-0-545-69032-4

Text copyright © 2015 by Abby Klein
Illustrations copyright © 2015 by John McKinley
All rights reserved. Published by Scholastic Inc.
SCHOLASTIC and associated logos are trademarks
and/or registered trademarks of Scholastic Inc.

12 11 10 9 8   16 17 18 19 20/0

Printed in the U.S.A.   40

First printing, January 2015

To Lumia,

One of Freddy's biggest fans.
Happy Snow Day!

Love,
A.K.

CHAPTERS

I have a problem.

A really, really big problem.

When we have a snow day, everyone
goes sledding on Cherry Hill. I love to
sled, but that hill is so steep, I'm
always afraid to go.

Let me tell you about it.

CHAPTER 1

Missing Mittens

"Freddy! Freddy!" my mom yelled from downstairs. "You are late. Let's go!"

I ran down to the kitchen.

"Finally," said my mom as she flipped sizzling bacon on the stove. "I've been calling you for the last ten minutes."

"Sorry, Mom," I said. "I can't find my mittens."

"Looks like you can't find your pants, either," said my sister, Suzie, laughing.

My mom turned around. "Freddy! What are you doing? Are you planning on going to school in your underwear?"

"I will give you five dollars if you go to school in your underwear," said Suzie. "I would definitely pay money to see that!"

"Ha-ha, very funny," I said. "I'm not going to school in my underwear."

"But you look so cute in your tighty-whities." Suzie chuckled.

"Freddy," said my dad, "you need to hurry up. I'm not driving you to school today if you miss your bus."

"But I need my mittens."

"Freddy, sit down and eat," said my mom.

"I can't eat right now."

"Why not? I'm making eggs. Do you want sunny-side up or scrambled?"

"I can't go to school without my blue shark mittens," I explained.

"Just wear the red ones," said my mom. "You had them yesterday."

"I bet you lost them," said Suzie. "Did you lose them? I think you lose a pair of mittens almost every week."

"I do not!"

"Do, too!"

"Do not!"

"Do, too!"

"All right, that's enough, you two," my dad interrupted. "Arguing is not helping Freddy get ready."

"Why don't you go back upstairs and finish getting dressed," said my mom.

"Yeah," said Suzie. "I think I'll lose my breakfast if I have to look at you eating in your underwear."

"After you put on some pants, check your

closet for the mittens," said my mom. "Maybe they're in there."

"Good thinking, Mom!" I called over my shoulder as I dashed out of the kitchen and up the stairs to my room.

I quickly put on a pair of pants and started rummaging around in my closet. It was such a mess that it was hard to find anything in there. I picked up stuff and threw it out into my room: my baseball glove, a blow-up shark from the aquarium, foam swords, a bug catcher, and my baseball bat.

"Uggghhhh! Where are those mittens?" I yelled.

Just then Suzie walked into my room. "Hey, watch where you're throwing that bat!"

"Watch where you're walking," I said.

"Oh, you are going to be in so much trouble," she said, looking around.

"No, I'm not."

"Yes, you are. You know how much Mom hates messes. She is a total neat freak."

"So?"

"So this is one giant mess!" said Suzie. "You are going to be late for school, *and* your room looks like a tornado hit it. You are in big T-R-O-U-B-L-E."

"Why are you even in here?" I hollered. "Get out!"

"Mom sent me up here to help you."

"Well, I don't need your help."

"It looks like you do if you want to find those mittens and not miss the bus."

She did have a point.

"Anyway, why do you need *those* mittens?" asked Suzie.

"Because it's supposed to snow today, so I need those mittens for recess."

"Why?"

"They don't get soaking wet when I play in the snow."

"What do you plan on doing?" asked Suzie.

"Making snowmen, building snow forts. You know. All that cool stuff."

"So do you want my help or not?" asked Suzie.

"Freddy!" my mom called. "The bus will be here in ten minutes."

"Looks like I don't have much choice," I mumbled.

"What's it worth to you?" said Suzie.

"I don't know."

"How about you make my bed for a week."

"A week! That is so unfair!"

"Take it or leave it," Suzie said, holding up her pinkie for a pinkie swear.

"Fine," I said as we locked pinkies. "But only if you find my mittens. Otherwise the deal is off."

"Excuse me," said Suzie, pushing me out of the way.

"Hey, watch it! You almost stepped on my toe."

"I said 'excuse me,'" said Suzie as she moved toward the closet.

"It's a waste of time looking in there," I said. "The mittens aren't there."

Suzie pushed some stuff around in my closet.

"Like I said. It's a waste of time."

Just then Suzie grabbed a coat out of the closet and stuffed her hands in the pockets.

"Well, lookee here," she said, grinning as she pulled the shark mittens out of the coat pockets.

"Where did you find those?"

"In this coat."

"Oh yeah," I said, slapping my forehead. "I forgot I took them to school earlier this year for show-and-tell."

"You're welcome," said Suzie.

"Yeah, thanks," I said. "You're the best sister in the whole world."

"I know," Suzie said.

"You want to help me get this stuff back in my closet?"

"Nope," said Suzie. "My job is done here. I'm going back down to finish my breakfast. But you'd better hurry, Freddy. You have to clean up this mess and make *two* beds. And you don't want to miss the bus."

CHAPTER 2

Snow, Snow, Snow!

"I think we are going to get some snow today," said our teacher, Miss Clark. "Does anyone know where snow comes from?" she asked.

"I do! I do!" Max yelled, jumping up out of his seat. "The sky!"

"Max," said Miss Clark, "you need to raise your hand quietly and stay in your seat if you want to be called on."

I raised my hand.

"Yes, Freddy. You have a quiet hand," said Miss Clark. "Do you know where snow comes from?"

"Yes, I do," I said.

"You do?" Jessie whispered.

"Yeah," I whispered back. "Robbie taught me." My best friend, Robbie, is a science genius. He knows everything about everything.

I turned to Miss Clark and said, "When the temperature drops below thirty-two degrees Fahrenheit, water freezes. The water droplets in the clouds then fall from the sky as snowflakes instead of raindrops."

"That is correct," said Miss Clark.

"Wow," Jessie whispered, "Robbie would be impressed."

"Thanks," I said and smiled.

"I love the snow," Max blurted out. "Snow is awesome!" He pumped his fist in the air.

"Max, please stop interrupting," said Miss Clark.

Chloe raised her hand.

"Yes, Chloe."

"I love the snow because then I get to wear my pink fluffy hat, and my pink fluffy mittens, and my pink fluffy coat!"

"Nobody cares, Pink Fluffy Girl!" barked Max.

Chloe stood up out of her seat and turned toward Max. "You take that back, you big meanie!"

"No way!" yelled Max.

Chloe stamped her foot. "Take it back right now!"

"Make me," said Max, making his hand into a fist.

"Chloe and Max," said Miss Clark, "we do not speak to each other that way. You both need to be more respectful. Please sit down in your seats."

"But —" Chloe started to say.

Miss Clark interrupted her. "I don't want to hear another word. Sit down now."

Chloe and Max glared at each other and sat back down.

"Now let's see . . . where was I?" said Miss Clark.

Jessie raised her hand. "We were talking about snow," said Jessie.

"Right, thank you, Jessie," said Miss Clark, "and Freddy just gave us a wonderful explanation about where snow comes from."

"I know something else interesting about snow," I said.

"Really?" said Miss Clark, smiling. "I would love to hear it."

"My friend Robbie told me that no two snowflakes are alike."

"No way! You just made that up," said Max.

"Actually, Freddy is right," said Miss Clark. "Every snowflake that falls from the sky is different from the last. You will never see two snowflakes that look exactly the same. Each snowflake is unique."

"That's what my nana says about me," said Chloe. "She says I'm unique."

"Of course she does," Jessie whispered to me.

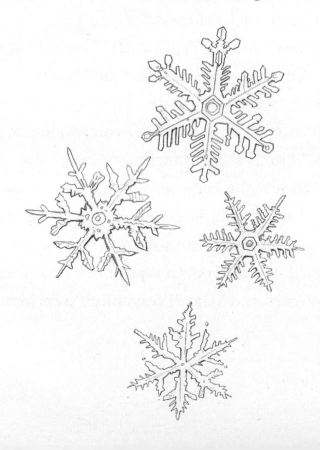

"She says that there is no one else in the world like me."

"That's for sure," I whispered back.

"Do you all know what a big snowstorm is called?" asked Miss Clark.

"A blizzard!" said Max. "My dad told me that when he was little, there was a huge blizzard. The snow piled up so high that he couldn't even open the front door!"

"Whoa!" I said. "That's crazy!"

"I can't even imagine that," said Jessie.

"Josh," said Miss Clark. "You are being so quiet. Do you have anything you would like to share with us about snow?"

"I don't really know anything about snow."

"What do you mean?" asked Miss Clark. "I'm sure you know lots of things."

"Well, I've never even seen snow," said Josh.

"What?" said Max. "Everybody's seen snow."

"Not me," said Josh. "Where I was living in California, there was no snow."

"No snow?" said Max.

"Yep," Josh said, nodding his head. "No snow."

"How do you have Christmas without snow?" said Chloe. "Haven't you ever heard of the song 'White Christmas'?"

"I've never had a white Christmas," said Josh. "Last year on Christmas it was eighty degrees."

"Eighty degrees!" said Jessie. "That's like summer."

"I think I even went surfing last Christmas." Josh laughed.

"That's so cool that you were at the beach in December," I said. "I don't think I've ever worn a bathing suit on Christmas."

Josh laughed again. "While you guys were making snowmen, I was making sandcastles."

"Well, you're in for a real treat," said Miss

Clark. "It is really quite beautiful when it snows."

"Yeah," I said. "Snow is awesome!"

"Recess is so much fun when it snows," said Jessie.

"Really?" said Josh.

"Oh yeah!" I said. "You can make snowmen, and build snow forts, and . . ."

"Make snow angels," said Jessie.

"Brrrr," Chloe said, pretending to shiver. "I don't like making snow angels. Sometimes the snow goes down your back, and it's so chilly."

"You are such a little fancypants," said Max. "Snow angels are the best!"

"Wow! That really does sound like fun," said Josh. "I can't wait!"

"Well, it looks like you won't have to wait too much longer," said Miss Clark.

I looked out the window. "Hey, guys, look!" I shouted. "It's started snowing!"

"Yes!" Max said, pumping his fist in the air.

"Woo-hoo!" Jessie said, doing a little dance and singing, "It's snowing. It's snowing."

"Get all of your gear on," said Miss Clark. "It's time for recess."

"Hurry up!" I said to Josh. "This is going to be the best recess ever!"

CHAPTER 3

The Challenge

"You were right, Freddy. This really is awesome," Josh shouted as he raced through the fresh snow.

"Wait for me!" I called after him.

Josh stopped, picked up some snow, and threw it in the air. "It's so light and fluffy."

I finally caught up with him. "Isn't it great? I knew you would love it."

Just then Robbie came running up. "Hey, guys, what's up?"

"Guess what?" I said.

"What?" said Robbie.

"Josh has never seen snow before."

"No way!" said Robbie.

"Yep. It's true," said Josh. "It never snowed where I lived in California."

"So what do you think?" asked Robbie.

"I think it's really sweet," said Josh.

"Sweet?" I repeated. "What do you mean? You're not eating it, are you?"

Josh laughed. "Oh, in California that means the same as awesome."

"Then I agree," I said. "The snow is sweet." We high-fived each other.

"Let's teach Josh how to make snow angels," said Robbie.

"Great idea!" I said. "Come here, Josh. Watch me."

I lay down in the snow and started sweeping my arms and legs up and down. "You just have to move your arms and legs like this."

Josh lay down in the snow next to me and did exactly what I was doing. He laughed. "This is fun!" he said.

"Now stick your tongue out and try to catch some snowflakes on it," I said.

"Okay," said Josh. He stuck his tongue out into the frozen air.

"Did you catch any?" I asked.

Just as I said that, I heard the voice. "Hey, what are you babies doing?"

I would know that voice anywhere. It was Max. Why did he always have to spoil our fun?

"I said, what are you babies doing?" he asked again.

"Go away," I mumbled into my scarf.

"What did you say, wimp?" Max asked as he pulled me up off the snow by my jacket.

"Nothing," I whispered.

"What? I can't hear you," Max said, tightening his grip on my collar.

Josh jumped up and came over to Max. "I'll tell you what he said. He said, go away."

I gulped. I couldn't believe Josh was taking on the biggest bully in the whole second grade.

"Oh really?" said Max, shaking a fist. "Is that what he said?"

Josh grabbed Max's hand.

"What are you doing?" Robbie whispered.

"I know what I'm doing," said Josh. "Max, let go of Freddy's jacket."

"Why should I?"

"Because I said so," said Josh. "You might scare other kids, but you don't scare me. Now let go of Freddy's jacket."

My heart was beating so fast I thought it was going to pop right out of my chest.

Max looked at me. Then he looked at Josh. Then back at me. Finally, he let go of my jacket.

"Whatever," he said.

I let out a big sigh. "Thank you," I mouthed to Josh.

"Max, no one is afraid of you," said Josh.

"That's not true," said Max. "Freddy's afraid of me."

"No, he's not."

"Oh yes, he is," said Max. "Freddy is just a little baby who is afraid of everything."

"Really?" said Josh. "I don't think Freddy is afraid of anything."

"Well, why don't you ask him about Cherry Hill?" said Max.

"Cherry Hill?" said Josh. "What's Cherry Hill?"

"It's the best sledding hill ever," said Max.

Josh laughed. "I don't think Freddy is afraid of a little hill."

"It's not a little hill," Max said, smiling. "It's a really big hill . . . the biggest hill around. And every year when we have a snow day, everyone goes sledding on Cherry Hill except for Freddy. The little baby is too afraid to go."

Josh looked at me. "I'm sure Freddy has gone down Cherry Hill a bunch of times."

I shook my head.

"See," said Max, flapping his elbows like a chicken. "Freddy's a chicken. *Cluck, cluck, cluck.* A big, fat chicken."

"Not this year," said Josh.

Max stopped clucking. "What do you mean?"

Yeah, I thought to myself. *What do you mean?*

"This year Freddy is going to go down Cherry Hill," said Josh.

"Is he crazy?" Robbie whispered to me.

"Uh-huh," I whispered back.

"Yeah, right," Max said, snickering. "I'll believe it when I see it."

"Well you'd better believe it, because you're going to see it," said Josh. "Right, Freddy?"

I stood there, frozen.

"Right, Freddy?" Josh said again.

"Right," I squeaked.

Max turned to me and smiled. "Freddy, I dare you to race me down Cherry Hill. What do you say?"

I opened my mouth, but no words came out.

"He'll be there. When's the race?" asked Josh.

"Tomorrow," said Max. "I heard it's supposed to be a snow day."

"Then we'll see you on Cherry Hill tomorrow," said Josh.

"Be prepared to lose," Max said, and started to walk away.

"Oh, Freddy won't lose," Josh called after Max. "You'll be the big loser. Just wait and see!"

CHAPTER 4

Are You Crazy?

"Are you crazy?" I said to Josh when Max was gone.

"What do you mean?" asked Josh.

"I've never gone down Cherry Hill in my life!" I said. "It's really steep."

"So?"

"So tomorrow I won't be able to race Max, and he's going to make fun of me in front of everybody and call me a baby like he always does."

"Why won't you be able to race Max?"

"I told you. The hill is too steep," I said. "I'm too afraid to go down it on my sled."

"Why?" asked Josh.

I pretended to knock on Josh's head. "Hello? Anybody in there? Are you listening to me? I said I'm afraid."

"It's all in your head," said Josh.

"What?"

"It's all in your head," Josh repeated.

"Can you speak English, please?" I said.

"You *think* you can't go down that hill, so you won't even try," said Josh.

"No, I *know* I can't," I said.

"Exactly," said Josh. "That's because you've convinced yourself you can't. When I was first learning to surf, I was just as scared of the waves as you are of Cherry Hill."

"Really?"

"Yep. Really."

"What did you do?"

"My dad told me what I'm telling you. He said, 'It's all in your head. You have to change your thinking.'"

"How do I do that?" I asked.

"You have to tell yourself that the hill isn't really that scary," Josh said.

"It is a big hill," said Robbie.

"And it is scary," I said.

"The waves were really big, too," said Josh, "and I was scared, but I just told myself that it probably wasn't as scary as I thought. My brain was making me think it was worse than it really was."

"Then what?" said Robbie.

"Then my dad told me to paddle out on my board. He said I had to face my fear, and then I would realize that it wasn't really so bad."

"Did you do it?" I asked.

"Yep. I got on my surfboard, and as I was paddling out, I just kept telling myself, *The waves are not that scary. I can do this. I can do this.*"

"Did talking to yourself work?"

"It did. When I changed my thinking, I felt my fears disappear, and the next thing I knew, I was riding my first wave!"

"Wow! That's awesome!" I said.

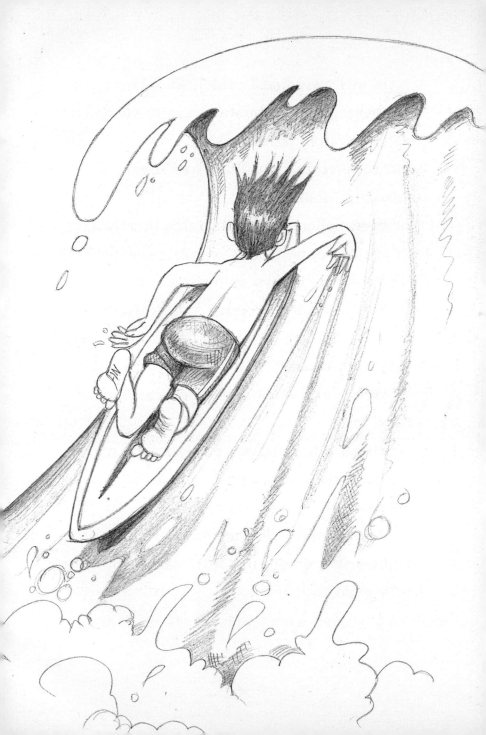

"It *was* awesome," said Josh. "After that, I was never afraid of the waves again. My dad was right. It was all in my head."

"So, Freddy, *you* have to change your thinking," said Robbie.

"It's worth a try," I said. "I don't really have a choice. If I don't race Max tomorrow, he'll call me a baby for the rest of my life."

"You can do it, Freddy," said Josh. "I know you can."

"You think so?"

"What's the worst thing that can happen?" asked Josh.

"I'll hit a huge bump, go flying off my sled, and do a giant face-plant in the snow."

"That's the *worst*?" said Josh.

"That sounds pretty terrible to me," I said.

"I think it sounds like fun," said Josh.

"You do?"

"Yeah. Flying down a hill like that, catching some air, and face-planting? I can't wait!"

"Like I said before, you're crazy."

"So you get a little snow in your face."

"A *lot* of snow in your face," I said, "and it's cold." I shivered just thinking about it.

"Just brush it off," said Josh, laughing. "Do you know how much water I've swallowed learning to surf?"

"How much?"

"Probably gallons and gallons. It's all part of learning not to be afraid, and how to take risks. I'm glad my dad didn't let me chicken out. Surfing is, like, my favorite thing to do, but I would never have learned if my dad let me walk away. I'm not going to let you walk away, either, Freddy."

"Josh, are you going to be there?" I asked.

"Of course I am," he said. "I wouldn't miss it."

"How about you, Robbie?"

"Freddy, you know I'm always there for you," said Robbie. "Josh and I will be cheering you on."

"We'll be screaming, 'Go, Freddy, go! Go, Freddy, go!'" said Josh.

"You really think I can do this?" I said to Josh.

"I know you can," said Josh. "You're not a baby. You're a cool kid."

I smiled. "You think I'm cool?"

"Yep," said Josh. "Really cool. Max just thinks he's cool, but he's not. You need to stop being so afraid of him."

"I can't help it. He's just so big and mean," I said.

"It's all in your head," Josh repeated. "It's all in your head."

"All right," I said, and gulped. "I'll do it. I'll race Max."

"He's going to be so surprised, he won't know what to do," said Robbie.

"Wait until Freddy wins the race," said Josh. "Then he *really* won't know what to do."

"I can't wait to see his face," said Robbie.

"Me, either," said Josh. "It's going to be great!"

I sighed.

"I just have one question, guys," said Josh.

"What?" Robbie and I said together.

"Where's Cherry Hill?"

We both laughed.

"It's on Potter's Farm."

"Where's that?"

We laughed again. "Just meet me at my house at ten o'clock tomorrow morning," I said to Josh.

"I can't wait!" said Josh. "My first snow day ever! Woo-hoo!"

CHAPTER 5

New Attitude

"Guess what?" I said that night at dinner.

"You learned how to spell your name today?" said Suzie.

"Oh, ha-ha! You think you're so funny, but you're not!"

Suzie grinned.

"What?" asked my dad.

"Do you know Josh has never seen snow? Can you believe it?"

"Never?" said my mom.

"Nope. Never. He said it didn't snow where he used to live in California."

"How can you have Christmas without snow?" said Suzie.

"He said that last Christmas he was on the beach, surfing and building sandcastles."

"So he was wearing a bathing suit, and you were wearing snow pants, boots, mittens, a hat, and a winter coat," said my mom. "That's funny."

"I know," I said. "Really funny."

"What did he think when he went out to recess today?" asked my dad.

"He loved the snow," I told him. "I taught him how to make snow angels."

"He didn't think it was too cold?" said my mom.

"No. He was even eating it right out of his gloves."

"I hope you told him not to eat yellow snow," said Suzie.

"EEEWWW! That's gross," I said. "I'm trying to eat dinner."

"Well, he's in for a real treat tomorrow," said my mom. "I think it's going to be a snow day."

"We're supposed to get about twelve inches tonight," said my dad. "I'd be surprised if you had school tomorrow."

I jumped out of my chair to do a happy dance. I sang, "It's a snow day! It's a snow day!" While I was dancing, I accidentally knocked over my glass of milk. A stream of milk raced across the table and into Suzie's lap.

She jumped up. "UGGGHHH! Now look what you've done, you big pain! I'm covered in milk."

I kept singing. "It's a snow day! It's a snow day!"

"Freddy," said my mom, "stop dancing and apologize to your sister."

"Oh, uh, sorry, Suzie," I said. "I'm just really excited."

"Now I have to go change before I can finish eating," said Suzie. "You are so annoying."

Suzie left the room, and my mom said,

"Freddy, go get a sponge to clean this up right now. What a mess!"

"It wouldn't be such a mess if we had a cat or a dog," I said. "They would just lick it all up."

"Nice try," said my dad. "But you know your mother is never going to agree to any pet other than a fish."

"Now go get a sponge," my mom said again, "unless *you* want to lick the milk off the floor."

I got down on my hands and knees and stuck out my tongue.

"Freddy!" my mom screamed. "I was just joking. Do not lick that milk off the floor."

I started to laugh. "I was just joking, too, Mom."

"Thank goodness," she said. "I was worried there for a minute. Now for the third time, go get a sponge!"

I went over to the sink, got a sponge, and came back to the table.

"Make sure you clean all of it up," said my mom. "I don't want Suzie sitting in a sticky chair."

Just then Suzie came back in the room. "Yeah, you'd better get all of it, Shark Breath. I don't want to have a sticky butt."

I wiped up the spill and sat back down.

"Thank you, Freddy, for cleaning that up," said my mom. "Now what were we talking about?"

"A snow day!" I said.

"Oh yes," said my mom. "How could I forget? You were doing a snow-day dance when this whole spill happened."

"So do you two have big plans for tomorrow?" asked my dad.

"Kimberly is going to come over, and we are going to stay inside and make some of those cool new bracelets everyone is wearing," said Suzie.

"You mean the ones with the colored rubber bands?" my mom said.

"Oh, those are really cool," I said. "Everyone in my class is wearing them."

"I know," said Suzie. "All the kids have them. Kimberly just got one of the kits to make them, so she's going to bring it over."

"Will you make one for me?" I asked Suzie.

"Maybe."

"Come on, Suzie," said my mom. "You can make one for Freddy."

"Not if he keeps dumping milk in my lap."

"That was an accident," I said.

"Well, if you weren't jumping around like a weirdo, those accidents wouldn't happen," Suzie said.

"How about you, Freddy?" asked my dad. "Do you have any plans?"

"I do," I said.

"I hope you plan to be outside. I remember when I had snow days as a kid," said my dad. "My favorite thing to do was to play in all the fresh snow. We'd make snowmen, and have snowball fights, and build snow forts."

"That's what I plan on doing," I said. "Josh and Robbie and I are going to do all of that stuff."

"Where?" asked my mom.

"On Potter's Farm."

"There's a great sledding hill over there," said my dad.

"Yeah. Cherry Hill," said Suzie. "But Freddy will never go sledding there."

"Why not?" asked my dad.

"Because it's steep, and he's too much of a scaredy-cat."

"I am not," I said.

"You are, too," said Suzie.

"Am not!"

"Are, too! Whenever we have a snow day, everyone goes sledding on Cherry Hill except you."

"Well, I'm definitely going this year," I said.

"Oh really?" said Suzie.

"Really," I said.

"Why will this year be any different?" she asked.

"Because of some advice Josh gave me."

"Josh?" said my mom. "But I thought he hasn't been sledding before."

"He hasn't, but he's a cool kid, and he gave me some cool advice."

"I like that attitude," said my dad.

"Yep. This year I will not chicken out," I said to my family, and then I whispered it again to myself, "I will not chicken out."

CHAPTER 6

Snow Day!

I woke up early the next morning, jumped out of bed, and ran to my window. Even though it was still dark out, all I could see was snow, snow, snow!

I raced to my parents' room. They were both sound asleep. My dad was snoring so loud it sounded like an airplane was roaring through their bedroom.

I poked my dad's shoulder. Nothing. I poked him again. This time a little harder.

"ZZZZZZZZZ." He snored even louder. I didn't think that was even possible.

I poked him one more time and yelled, "Hey, Dad, wake up!"

He sat up in bed with a start. "Huh? What? What's going on? Is something wrong?"

I laughed. "No, nothing's wrong."

He squinted at the time on the clock. "Then why are you waking me up at five o'clock in the morning?"

"Because I want to know if it's a snow day today," I said.

My mom opened her eyes. "What's going on? Is something wrong, Freddy?"

"No, nothing's wrong."

"Then why are you in here?"

I sighed. "Like I said to Dad, I want to know if it's a snow day."

"You couldn't wait until later to ask us this?" said my dad. "The sun isn't even up yet."

"I just want to know," I said.

"Well, we have no idea," said my mom. "We haven't checked the school closings on the news channel."

"Can you check it now?" I asked impatiently.

"If we do, will you let us go back to sleep?" asked my dad.

"Yes. You can sleep as long as you want!" I said.

My dad grabbed the remote and turned on the television. I sat down on my parents' bed.

"Do you see it? Do you see it?" I asked, bouncing up and down on the bed.

"Freddy, calm down," said my mom. "Stop bouncing. We have to get to the right channel first."

"But I'm just so excited," I said.

My dad changed the channel, and a list of school closings was scrolling across the screen.

"Is Lincoln Elementary on that list?"

"I'm looking," said my dad.

It seemed like it was taking forever.

"Oh, there it is," said my mom. "Lincoln Elementary is closed today."

"Woo-hoo!" I shouted. I hopped up and started jumping up and down on the bed. "It's a snow day! It's a snow day!"

"Freddy!" said my mom. "Get down right now. You know you're not supposed to jump on the beds."

"Sorry, Mom. I just got carried away." I bounced off the bed.

"Why don't you go back to sleep," said my mom.

"Are you kidding? I can't sleep now."

"Well, we can," said my dad. "You promised

you'd let us go back to sleep once we got you the information."

"Okeydokey," I said, walking out of the room. "I'm going."

I went back to my room, sat down on my bed, and looked at the clock. It said 5:15. I had to wait almost five hours before Josh and Robbie came over. I didn't know if I could wait that long.

I decided to look for all of my snow gear just to make sure I wasn't missing anything.

I bounded down the stairs to the mudroom. I found my snow pants, my boots, my shark hat, my shark mittens, and my coat. Something was missing. What was it?

Oh yes! My long underwear and my neck gaiter.

I raced back upstairs to my room and opened all my dresser drawers. I dug through every drawer. I found my neck gaiter mixed in with

my bathing suits, but I couldn't find my long underwear.

I sat down on my bed and hit my forehead with the palm of my hand. "Think, think, think," I whispered to myself.

Maybe Mom put it in Suzie's room by accident, I thought.

I ran into Suzie's room and started going through her drawers. I was trying to be quiet, but Suzie woke up.

"What do you think you're doing?" she asked.

"Looking for something."

"Why are you in my room?"

"Because I think it might be in here."

"Why would something of yours be in *my* room?" Suzie asked.

"Maybe Mom put it in here by accident."

"What are you looking for?"

"My long underwear."

"Long underwear?" said Suzie. "Unless you want pink underwear with flowers on it, you're not going to find any long underwear in here."

"I just have to be sure."

"Well, I'm sure," said Suzie. "It's not in here."

I ignored her and started throwing things out of her drawer. A pair of purple undies hit her in the face.

"That's it!" Suzie yelled. "Get out! Get out right now!"

"But —" I started to say.

"O-U-T, out!" Suzie shouted, pushing me out the door. She slammed the door behind me.

Where else could I look? I couldn't go back into my parents' room and ask my mom. I promised her that I would let them sleep.

I guessed there was nothing else to do but wait.

If only I could make time fly.

CHAPTER 7

Ready, Freddy?

Time moved slower than a snail, but at last it was ten o'clock.

My mom had found my long underwear, so I was all dressed and ready to go.

"Freddy," said my mom, "why don't you take off your coat until your friends come? You must be sweating like crazy."

"That's okay, Mom. They'll be here any

minute, and I don't want to waste any time getting out the door."

Suzie walked into the room. "Is Kimberly here yet?"

"Oh yeah," I said. "She came two hours ago, but I forgot to tell you."

"You think you're so funny," said Suzie. "Don't you?"

Just then the doorbell rang.

Suzie reached for the door, but I jumped in front of her and grabbed the handle to open it.

Robbie and his sister, Kimberly, had picked up Josh on their way over.

"Hi, guys!" I said.

Kimberly stepped inside, and I joined my friends outside.

"You guys ready to go?" I asked.

"You bet!" said Robbie.

"I've been ready since six o'clock," said Josh.

I laughed. "I got up at five this morning!"

"This is going to be the best day ever," said Josh. "I've never had a snow day before. So far, it's pretty sweet . . . no school *and* tons of snow to play in!"

"Let's get going," said Robbie. "We don't want to waste a minute."

We grabbed our sleds, walked down the driveway, and turned right down the street.

When we came to Mrs. Golden's house, her dog, Baxter, was rolling around in the snow in the front yard. He ran over to me as we walked by.

"Hey, Baxter. What do you think, boy? It looks like you like the snow as much as we do."

Baxter barked, and we all laughed.

"See you later, boy. Have fun making your doggy snow angels," I said as I gave him one last pat on the head.

"So how far is it to Potter's Farm?" Josh asked.

"Not too far," I said.

"It's only about a ten-minute walk," said Robbie.

All of a sudden, I felt a snowball hit the back of my jacket.

"Hey!" I said, turning around. "Where did that come from?"

Josh laughed and took off running down the street. "Betcha can't catch me," he said.

I grabbed a handful of snow and pressed it into a ball as I ran after him. When I got close enough, I threw it with all my might, and it hit him square on the back of the head.

"Wow! Nice arm," Josh said. "I didn't know you could throw like that. You must play baseball."

Robbie threw two snowballs, one right after the other, and caught us both by surprise.

"That was pretty sneaky, Robbie," I said. "You just popped out of nowhere."

We continued chasing each other and throwing snowballs all the way to Potter's Farm.

By the time we reached the farm, we were all out of breath. I threw my sled on the ground. "Hang on a second, guys," I said. "I've got to catch my breath."

"Me, too," said Robbie.

"I thought you guys said it was a ten-minute walk," said Josh. "That didn't seem like ten minutes."

"That's because we ran the whole way," I said.

"Let's hit the sledding hill," said Josh. "I've been waiting to go sledding all morning."

"Nah, let's make a snow fort first," I said.

"How do you do that?" asked Josh.

"You have to pack the snow into bricks, like this," said Robbie, making a rectangular block of snow, "and then you stack the bricks like an igloo."

"That's pretty cool," said Josh. "Where should we do it?"

"How about over by that tree?" said Robbie.

"That's a great place!" I said.

We ran over to the tree, put our sleds down, and started making blocks of snow. We stacked them one on top of another.

Josh looked around. "I see a lot of kids here, but I don't see Max."

"Really?" I said, pretending that I hadn't noticed until he said something. Secretly, I was hoping that Max wouldn't come, and I wouldn't have to race him.

Just then Jessie walked up. "Hi, guys," she said.

"Hey, Jessie," I said. "Want to help?"

"Sure, Freddy!"

"Jessie, have you seen Max?" asked Josh.

"No, I don't think he's here," said Jessie. "I actually hope that big bully doesn't come."

"I hope he does," said Josh.

"You do?" said Jessie. "Why?"

"Because Freddy is going to beat the pants off of him."

"Freddy? Really? What are you talking about?" Jessie asked.

"Freddy and Max are going to race down Cherry Hill," said Josh.

"You are, Freddy?" said Jessie. "But aren't you afraid of Cherry Hill?"

"*Was* afraid," said Josh, smiling, "but not anymore. Freddy has changed his thinking."

"Wow, Freddy! That's great!" said Jessie.

"Yeah, great!" I mumbled. My heart was starting to beat faster just thinking about it.

"Now I *do* hope Max shows up," said Jessie.

All of a sudden, I heard a familiar voice behind me. "Well, then, it's your lucky day, because here I am," said Max, grinning.

He grabbed me by my jacket and spun me around. "Ready to race, wimp, or you too scared?"

"Oh, no, he's ready," said Josh.

"I want to hear it from him," said Max.

I gulped. "Ready."

"Then let's race!"

CHAPTER 8

Ready, Set, Race!

Max picked up his sled and took off running toward Cherry Hill.

My feet wouldn't move. It felt like they were frozen into the ground.

"Come on, Freddy. What are you waiting for?" asked Josh.

"I don't know if I can do this," I said.

"What do you mean? Of course you can," said Josh. "Remember, it's all in your head."

I nodded.

"Change your thinking," said Robbie.

"After this race, Max will never be able to call you a baby again," said Jessie.

I gulped. "You guys really think I can do this?"

"Yes!" they all said together. "We know you can."

We high-fived one another. "You guys are the best friends ever!" I said.

"Let's get going before Max thinks you chickened out," said Josh.

We grabbed our sleds and ran toward the hill. As we got closer, it looked even steeper than I remembered it.

"It's all in your head. It's all in your head," I whispered to myself.

"There you guys are," said Max. "I couldn't see you. I thought the little baby had chickened out at the last minute like he always does."

"Are you crazy?" said Josh. "Freddy's been waiting for this race all morning."

"Oh really?" said Max, grinning.

"Yeah. Really," said Josh.

"Then let's get going," said Max. "What are we waiting for?"

We slowly climbed to the top of Cherry Hill.

"Okay, here are the rules," said Josh.

"We don't need any dumb rules," said Max.

"Yes, you do," said Josh, "so listen up. Rule Number One: No one starts until I say 'go!' Rule Number Two: You cannot crash into the other person's sled on purpose. And Rule Number Three: The first person to cross the finish line is the winner."

"Where's the finish line?" asked Max.

"You see that big tree over there?" said Josh.

"You mean the one with the crooked branches?" I said.

"Yep. That's the one. The first person to pass that tree is the winner."

"Easy peasy," said Max.

"All right. Get on your sleds," said Josh.

I put my sled in the snow and sat down on it. I could feel my palms sweating in my mittens. My heart was racing.

"It's all in your head. It's all in your head," I told myself over and over.

Josh bent down and whispered in my ear, "Face your fear, Freddy. You can do this."

"Hey! What are you telling him?" shouted Max. "You can't make any secret plans. That's cheating!"

"Calm down over there," said Josh. "We're not making any secret plans."

"Ready, Freddy?" Josh whispered.

I nodded.

Josh stood up. "Get ready, get set, go!"

I gave my sled a little push, pulled my legs in, and we were off!

My sled was practically flying down the hill. The wind stung my eyes. The trees were whizzing by so fast they were a blur. I couldn't see Max anywhere.

I hit a huge bump, and my sled flew into the air. I hung on to the sides of the sled with all my might and held my breath. The sled hit the frozen ground again and continued on down the hill.

The big tree was getting closer and closer.

I could hear my friends chanting, "Go, Freddy, go! Go, Freddy, go!"

A smile crossed my face. Maybe I was actually going to win this race.

Then, out of nowhere, Max flew by me on his sled.

My heart sank.

Max turned around and yelled, "See you later, loser!"

Turning around to brag like that was a big mistake. He didn't see a huge bump directly in his path. His sled hit the bump, and Max went flying through the air.

He landed face-first in the snow, just as my sled crossed the finish line.

My friends all came running over.

Josh picked me up and swung me around. "You did it, Freddy! You did it!"

"You won the race!" said Robbie.

"You beat the biggest bully in the whole second grade," said Jessie.

I still couldn't believe it. I beat Max in a race down Cherry Hill!

Josh walked over to Max, who was lying on the ground covered in snow from head to toe. "Who's the loser now?" said Josh.

"Yeah. Whatever," Max mumbled.

"Not 'whatever,'" said Josh. "Freddy won fair and square. You need to congratulate him."

Max looked up at me with snow still clinging to his eyelashes. "Congratulations, you little baby," he grumbled.

"You can't call him that ever again," said Jessie. "Not after that race."

"Fine. Congratulations," Max mumbled again.

I smiled. *I did it*, I thought to myself. *I changed my thinking and faced my fear, just like Josh had taught me. I beat Max Sellars in a race down Cherry Hill.*

"So what did you think?" asked Josh. "It wasn't so bad, was it?"

"No! It was sweet! Really sweet!" I said.

We laughed.

"I'm ready to do it all over again," I said.

"Then what are we waiting for?" said Josh. "Let's go!"

Freddy's Fun Pages

SNOW DOUGH

Want to have some fun with snow indoors? Make this snow dough and then build your own snowman. The best part is he won't melt!

DIRECTIONS:

1. Mix together in a pan until smooth:

    2 cups flour

    2 cups salt

    2 tbsp cream of tartar

    2 tbsp vegetable oil

    2 cups water

2. With a grown-up's help, cook over medium heat, stirring constantly until the mixture forms a ball and sticks to the spoon.

3. Cool and knead in iridescent glitter to make it sparkle.

4. Build your snowman!

(Store your snow dough in an airtight container)

MAKE A SNOW SCENE

Do you like to play in the snow like Freddy when you have a snow day? Try this special craft to illustrate your favorite snow day activity!

YOU WILL NEED:

1. Blue construction paper
2. Crayons or markers
3. White paint
4. Q-tips

On a piece of the blue construction paper, draw your favorite snow day activity with markers or crayons.

Dip a Q-tip into the white paint and dot it all over your picture to make it snow!

WINTER SCIENCE EXPERIMENT

Try this fun and easy science experiment to learn more about freezing and melting.

YOU WILL NEED:

a clear plastic cup
water
a stopwatch or a timer

DIRECTIONS:

1. Fill the cup halfway up with water
2. Predict how many minutes it will take the water to freeze
3. Place the cup of water in your freezer and use your stopwatch to time exactly how many minutes it takes for the water to freeze
4. Once it is completely frozen, take the cup out of the freezer

5. Predict how many minutes it will take the ice to melt

6. Use your stopwatch to time exactly how many minutes it takes for the ice to melt

7. Which took longer . . . freezing or melting?

Have you read all about Freddy?

Second Grade!

Don't miss any of Freddy's funny adventures!